Dear Parent:
Your child's love of reading starts here!

Every child learns to read in a different way and at his or her own speed. You can help your young reader improve and become more confident by encouraging his or her own interests and abilities. You can also guide your child's spiritual development by reading stories with biblical values and Bible stories, like I Can Read! books published by Zonderkidz. From books your child reads with you to the first books he or she reads alone, there are I Can Read! books for every stage of reading:

SHARED READING
Basic language, word repetition, and whimsical illustrations, ideal for sharing with your emergent reader.

BEGINNING READING
Short sentences, familiar words, and simple concepts for children eager to read on their own.

READING WITH HELP
Engaging stories, longer sentences, and language play for developing readers.

READING ALONE
Complex plots, challenging vocabulary, and high-interest topics for the independent reader.

ADVANCED READING
Short paragraphs, chapters, perfect bridge to chapter bc

I Can Read! books have introduced chil   ce 1957. Featuring award-winning authors and il   fabulous cast of beloved characters, I Can Read! books   for beginning readers.

A lifetime of discovery begins with the magical words **"I Can Read!"**

Visit www.icanread.com for information on enriching your child's reading experience.
Visit www.zonderkidz.com for more Zonderkidz I Can Read! titles.

A friend loves at all times.
He is there to help when trouble comes.
—*Proverbs 17:17*

Barnabas Helps a Friend
Copyright © 2008 by Amaze Entertainment, Inc.
Illustrations copyright © 2008 by Amaze Entertainment, Inc.

Requests for information should be addressed to:
Zonderkidz, Grand Rapids, Michigan 49530

Library of Congress Cataloging-in-Publication Data

Lepp, Royden, 1980-
   Barnabas helps a friend / story by Royden Lepp ; pictures by Royden Lepp.
      p. cm. – (I can read! My first)
      Summary: When a big storm destroys Mr. Beaver's home, Barnabas Bear and his friends work together and repair the damage.
     ISBN-13: 978-0-310-71585-6 (softcover)
     ISBN-10: 0-310-71585-7 (softcover)
     [1. Bears–Fiction. 2. Animals–Fiction. 3. Cooperativeness–Fiction. 4. Storms–Fiction.]
I. Title.
PZ7.L5557Bh 2008
[E]–dc22

            2007022906

Art Direction: Jody Langley
Cover Design: Sarah Molegraaf

Printed in China

08 09 10 • 4 3 2 1

ZONDERkidz

I Can Read!™

SHARED
My First
READING

Barnabas Helps a Friend

story and pictures by

Royden Lepp

Barnabas looked out of his den.

Rain poured down.

Lightning lit up the sky.

"This is a bad storm,"
Barnabas said.

Soon the storm ended.

The storm had made a mess
of Brookdale Wood.

"I will go see if my friends
need my help," Barnabas said.

Barnabas saw his best friend.
"Hi, Russell Raccoon," he said.
"Are you okay?"

Russell nodded his head yes.
"Let's go see if our friends
need help," Barnabas said.

Mr. Beaver was very sad.

"What happened, Mr. B?"

Barnabas asked.

"The wind blew very hard.
A tree fell down on my house,"
said Mr. Beaver.

"I will fix my house,"
Mr. B. said.
"I'm good with wood."

"We will help," said Barnabas.
"Friends always help
when trouble comes."

"Thanks," Mr. Beaver said.

"Let's move this tree first."

The friends pushed and pulled.

They tugged and tugged,
but that tree did not move.

"This is too hard.
I'll start a new house
tomorrow," said Mr. B.

Mr. B. sat down on a rock.
Barnabas and Russell
walked away sadly.

"You know what we can do?"
Barnabas said to Russell.

"Let's ask our friends
to help fix Mr. B.'s house.
We can do it all together."

Barnabas and Russell asked
Timothy Turtle to help them.

"I'm busy," said Timothy.

"I'm sorry."

"That's okay," Barnabas said.

Barnabas and Russell asked
Sadie Squirrel to help them.

"I'd love to," said Sadie.

"But I am helping someone."

"Oh, I see," Barnabas said.

Barnabas and Russell looked
and looked for more friends.

"We can fix Mr. B.'s house,"
Barnabas said.
"We can do it together."

Barnabas and Russell Raccoon
went back to Mr. B.'s house.
They were so surprised!

They found all their friends
helping Mr. Beaver clean up.

Everyone helped move the tree
off Mr. Beaver's house.

"Yippee!" they shouted.

The friends of Brookdale Wood

worked together

to fix Mr. Beaver's house.

"I'm glad that everyone
is helping Mr. Beaver,"
said Barnabas.

"Of course," said Timothy.
"Friends always help
when trouble comes."